專門替中國人寫的英文課本

中級本（下冊）

He is bored.

從蜻蜓點水到小題大做

李家同

　　這兩本書是《專門替中國人寫的英文課本》的中級本，比起初級本來，這兩本當然高級多了，至少讀了這兩本書以後，我們可以學會如何使用現在完成式、過去完成式、過去進行式、被動語氣以及其他相當重要的英文基本規則。

　　就以現在完成式為例，我曾經看過目前很多國中英文教科書如何介紹這種觀念的，他們的介紹方法很簡單，在一篇文章中間，有很多很多的句子用的都是現在完成式，然後在文章的後面，會有一兩個例子，介紹過去分詞(past participle)，也介紹一下現在完成式的定義，這一下就大功告成矣。

　　什麼情況之下，要用現在完成式，這些教科書無法解釋，這些書的作者當然知道什麼情況之下要用現在完成式，但是他們不能在英文教科書裡用中文解釋觀念，當然又不能用英文解釋，因為畢竟這些書都是寫給小孩子看的，你用英文解釋現在完成式的用法，誰看得懂呢？

　　這本書的最大優點，就是在於它痛痛快快地用中文解釋英文的基本規則，我一直在想，如果不這樣做，如何能教好英文？英文不是那麼簡單的，我敢說，很多人一輩子弄不清楚現在式的意義，我們其實是不能輕易用現在式的，可是我們卻會不停地犯錯，濫用現在式。為什麼？還不是因為我們沒有在入門的英文教科書中將現在式解釋清楚。

　　大多數的英文教科書，因為不能用中文解釋，對於任何英文的基本規則，都只好蜻蜓點水一樣地輕輕帶過，有些重要的議題，甚至在書中一字不提，難

怪我國很多學生到了大學,寫英文句子仍然是錯誤百出。

這本書的作風正好相反,作者對於每一個英文規則,都詳加解釋,以人稱代名詞的受格而言,就整整講了一課,如果一位同學忽然之間對於這方面弄不清楚了,可以翻到這一課來,我們可以保證他一定會找到所要的資料。

讀英文,就要勤加練習,這本書的另一優點是練習題奇多,任何同學做了這麼多的練習題,當然都會對這些規則很熟悉了。

但是,學英文,總會犯錯的,所以這本書就設計了很多改錯的練習題。大家千萬不要小看了這些改錯習題,很多大學生進了研究所,甚至已經是博士班學生了,仍然在犯這些錯。如果這些大學生當年做過這類改錯的題目,情形一定會好得多。

這兩本書裡仍有中翻英的練習題,這是十分值得讚揚的。我們初學英文,不可能一開始就想英文句子的,我們當然會從中文句子想起,所以練習中翻英是有其必要的。最重要的是,一旦學生會將很多中文句子翻成英文,他的信心一定會大增,因為他會有相當好的成就感。舉例來說,如果你請學生翻譯「我從未去過台南。」,他脫口而出 "I have never been to Tainan.",試問他會多快樂。

這兩本書裡有整段的文章出現,有趣的是,這些文章都有解釋的,這恐怕也是創舉,我沒有看到別的英文教科書有這種做法。

目次

第十三課

過去完成式

He hadn't called his friends before he met them.

在上冊第十一課裡，我們將「現在完成式」與「過去式」兩相對照，讀者應該明白兩者雖然都發生在過去，但不一樣的地方在於：「過去式」通常表明過去特定的時間（如：two years ago, last night, at 3:00P.M.）所發生的事；「現在完成式」則用來表達過去的經驗。

本課我們將「過去完成式」和「過去式對比」，如果將「過去完成式」和「過去式」放在同一時間軸來看，我們會發現兩者都是過去發生的事，但若某個事情或行為比過去式更早發生，而且有「完成」的意思，則要用「過去完成式」來表示。如果是兩件清清楚楚發生在過去的行為或事情，則都用「過去式」比較妥當。

例如：

Before I washed my face, I brushed my teeth.（我先刷牙，再洗臉。）

過去完成式是 had + 動詞第三態變化（過去分詞）。

例如：I wasn't hungry because I had just eaten.（我不餓，因為我剛吃過。）

13-1 生字

hungry	餓
because	因為
eat	吃 (eat, ate, eaten)
already	已經
finish	完成 (finish, finished, finished)
meet	見面 (meet, met, met)
writer	作家
send	寄 (send, sent, sent)
Canada	加拿大
learn	學習 (learn, learned, learned)
late	晚
party	派對
by the time	之前 (by the time = before)
most	大多數的
guest	客人
train	火車
leave	離開 (leave, left, left)

13-2 課文

Yesterday they were hungry because they had not eaten for four hours.

昨天他們很餓，因為他們已經 4 小時沒有吃。

Before I went to bed last night, I had already finished my homework.

昨晚我上床前，我已經寫完功課了。

Before he met the writer, he had sent an e-mail to her.

他跟這位作家見面之前，先寄了伊媚兒給她。

Before she went to Canada, she had learned some English.

她去加拿大之前，學了一些英文。

After he had heard the news, he ran out.

他聽到這個消息後跑了出去。

We were late. The party had already started.

我們來晚了。這個派對已經開始了。

By the time I left the party, most guests had already gone.

等我離開派對時，多數的客人已經走了。

By the time the students arrived, the class had already finished.

等學生到了，課已經結束了。

13-2-1 because 因為

She didn't go with us because she had been there before.

她沒有跟我們去，因為她以前去過那裡了。

Yesterday I didn't eat mangos because I had already eaten too many.

昨天我沒有吃芒果，因為我已經吃太多了。

Last night I didn't watch the news on TV because I had already heard the news.

昨晚我沒有看電視新聞，因為我已經聽過新聞了。

＊注意：hear（聽），它的三態變化是 hear, heard, heard。

 13-2-2 before 在……之前

Before he saw the movie, he had already known the story.

他看電影之前，已經知道這個故事了。

Before the boss came, they had already finished all the work.

老闆來之前，他們已經把全部的工作做完了。

Before he called me, he had read my novel.

他打電話給我之前，已經讀了我的小說。

 13-2-3 after 在……之後

After he had finished his homework, he went home.

他做完功課後就回家。

After I had read her novel, I sent an e-mail to her.

我讀了她的小說之後，寄了伊媚兒給她。

After she had heard the good news, she called her mom.

她知道這個好消息後，就打電話給她母親。

 13-3 縮寫

I had written a letter. → I'd written a letter.

You had finished your work. → You'd finished your work.

He had met her. → He'd met her.

She had studied. → She'd studied.

It had eaten. → It'd eaten.

We had heard the news. → We'd heard the news.

You had left. → You'd left.

They had known my name. → They'd known my name.

13-4-1 請將下列兩個句子用 before 或 after 連接起來，記得其中有一句要用過去完成式。

例：　I wrote a letter to her at 7:00 P.M.　I went to bed at 10:00 P.M.
　　→ Before I went to bed, I had written a letter to her.

1.　I finished reading a novel at 11:00 P.M.　I went to bed at 12:00 P.M.

　　_____

2.　My brother learned English last year.　My brother went to America this year.

　　_____

3.　My mother did the dishes at 8:00 P.M.　My mother read a novel at 9:00 P.M.

　　_____

4.　She finished her work at 7:00 P.M.　She wrote a letter.

　　_____

5.　David called his father at 6:00 P.M.　David went home at 7:00 P.M.

　　_____

6.　The teacher had lunch at 12:00 P.M.　The teacher took a nap at 1:00 P.M.

　　_____

7.　My grandma made cookies at 2:00 P.M.　My grandma made a cake at 4:00 P.M.

_____

8.   My sister finished her homework at 7:00 P.M. the day before yesterday. My sister went to school at 8:00 A.M. yesterday.

_____

9.   Those students arrived at 9:00 P.M. The English class finished at 8:45 P.M.

_____

10.   My grandfather saw a movie at 3:00 P.M. My grandfather wrote letters to his friends at 5:00 P.M.

_____

13-4-2 填填看

1.   Amy _____ (finish) reading the book before she went to school.

2.   My sister _____ (write) a letter before she met her friend.

3.   My friend had bought a house before he _____ (move 搬到) to Taipei.

4.   My parents _____ (call) my teacher before they met her.

5.   They had gone to bed _____ he came home at 11:00P.M.

6.   My brother and I played computer games _____ we had finished our homework.

7.   I _____ (finish) my homework before I watched TV.

8.   My mother had cleaned the kitchen（廚房）_____ she made a cake.

9.   My cats didn't _____ any milk because they had been ill（病了）.

10. My cousin had done the dishes _____ she went to bed.
11. Amy had been to America _____ she learned English.
12. I _____ (finish) my homework before I went to school.
13. She didn't say a word after I _____ (meet) her.
14. She _____ (leave) after she had finished her work.
15. Tom _____ (call) his teacher because he hadn't gone to school.

13-4-3 英文該怎麼說？

1. 他來台灣之前已經學了一些中文(learned some Chinese)。

   _____

2. 我見新老師之前先買了一個禮物(bought a present)。

   _____

3. 我睡覺之前已經先寫完了功課。

   _____

4. 我的哥哥們打掃完他們的臥房(clean their bedroom)後再上學。

   _____

5. 我昨晚不餓，因為已經吃過了晚餐。

   _____

6. 去年他搬到(moved)台北(Taipei)之前，已經在台中(Taichung)住過3年。

   _____

7. 我的朋友和我先寫完了功課(finished our homework)再看電視。

   _____

8. 我的祖母吃過早飯之後去了公園(went to the park)。

   _____

9.   我的學生先讀了書再上學。

_____

10.   他看電影之前已經先讀過了小說。

_____

13-4-4 改錯

1.   I have finished my homework before I went to bed.
2.   I was late. The class had already start.
3.   We didn't go because we had already knew the story.
4.   I see the movie before I watched TV.
5.   What have she done before she met her English teacher?
6.   My grandpa was late. The movie already started.
7.   By the time I arrive, the bus had gone.
8.   After she came to Taiwan, she had learned some Chinese.（中文）
9.   My cats are hungry because they hadn't eaten for two days.
10.   After I met her, I had already read her novel.

第十四課

過去進行式

When you called me,
I was washing my face.

我們在初級本談過現在進行式是用來表現現在正在發生的事，例如：I am washing my face now.（我現在正在洗臉。）

本課要談的「過去進行式」，則是用來表現過去某段時間正在做的事。例如：

I was washing my face at 6:00 P.M. last night.

有時我們會問：「昨晚我打電話給你的時候，你在做什麼？」昨晚我打電話是用過去式，你在做什麼則要用過去進行式。例如：

· Last night when I called you, what were you doing?

　昨晚當我打電話給你時，你正在做什麼？

· When you called me, I was taking a shower.

　當你打電話給我時，我正在洗澡。

14-1 生字

when	當⋯⋯時候
was taking a shower	那時候正在洗澡（淋浴）
was making the bed	那時候正在鋪床
was playing the piano	那時候正在彈鋼琴
was doing my homework	那時候正在寫功課
was drinking coffee	那時候正在喝咖啡
was combing my hair	那時候正在梳頭髮
were sleeping	那時候正在睡覺
were taking a nap	那時候正在小睡片刻
were doing the dishes	那時候正在洗碗

＊記得嗎？I, she, he, it 後面接 was ，we, you, they 後面接 were 。（was 是 am, is 的過去式，were 是 are 的過去式。）

What were you doing at 9:00 P.M. yesterday?

昨天晚上 9 點你在做什麼？

I was taking a shower.

我正在洗澡。

What were you doing at 7:00 A.M.?

(今天)早上 7 點你在做什麼？

I was making my bed.

我正在鋪床。

What was your sister doing when I called her last night?

昨晚我打電話給你姊姊的時候，她正在做什麼？

She was playing the piano.

她正在彈鋼琴。

What was your brother doing when you came home last night?

昨晚你回家時，你的哥哥在做什麼？

He was doing his homework.

他正在寫功課。

What was your mom doing when you went to school this morning?

今天早上你上學時，你的媽媽在做什麼？

She was drinking coffee.

她正在喝咖啡。

What was your sister doing at 8:00 A.M. today?

今天早上8點你的姊姊在做什麼？

She was combing her hair. (＊注意：combing 的 b 不發音)

她正在梳頭髮。

What were your cats doing when you went out in the afternoon?

今天下午你出去時，你的貓在做什麼？

They were all sleeping.

牠們都在睡覺。

What were your parents doing when you came home?

你回家時，你的父母在做什麼？

They were taking a nap.

他們在睡午覺。

What were you doing when your mom came home last night?

你媽媽回家時你們在做什麼？

We were doing the dishes.

我們正在洗碗。

 14-2-1 圖表

I	was	brushing my teeth	at 7:00 A.M.	yesterday.
You	were	combing your hair	at 8:00 A.M.	yesterday.
He	was	washing his face	at 6:00 A.M.	yesterday.
She	was	washing her hands	at 3:00 P.M.	yesterday.
It	was	drinking milk	at 5:00 P.M.	yesterday.
We	were	doing the dishes	at 1:00 P.M.	yesterday.
You	were	making your beds	at 9:00 P.M.	yesterday.
They	were	taking a nap	at 3:00 P.M.	yesterday.

14-3 練習題

14-3-1 請回想一下，昨天早上 6 點、10 點、下午 3 點、晚上 7 點、11 點你在做什麼？

1. I _____ at 6:00 A.M.
2. I _____ at 10:00 A.M.
3. I _____ at 3:00 P.M.
4. I _____ at 7:00 P.M.
5. I _____ at 11:00 P.M.

14-3-2 填填看：

1. I _____ (learn) English for three years.
2. Tom didn't _____ (study) English last night.
3. He _____ (take) a shower when his friend called him.
4. I never met him after he_____ (go) to China.
5. Her grandma _____ (have) a cell phone.
6. Who _____ (be) your English teacher next year?
7. When you called me last night, I _____ (do) the dishes.
8. I _____ (buy) a bicycle before I went to America.
9. He didn't like this book after he _____ (talk) to his teacher.
10. She _____ (decide) to live in Tainan after she had read that book.

11. What were you_____ (do) when I came to see you last night?

12. The boy _____ (make) his bed when his mom came home.

13. When I came home, my mom _____ (read) a novel.

14. His grandpa _____ (find) a dog in the park last week.

15. His cousin doesn't _____ (care) about his health.

14-3-3 改錯

1. I wasn't take a shower when you called me last night.
2. She isn't combing her hair when I got up.
3. He was study English when you came to see him.
4. I was sleep at 2:00 this morning.
5. You are eating breakfast when I talked to her.
6. Her mom was takeing a nap when I called her.
7. Her friends wasn't playing soccer when their teacher called them.
8. I didn't playing the piano when you came.
9. Amy wasn't read a novel when you called her.
10. What are you doing when I got up this morning?

第十五課

主動語態和被動語態

This picture was painted by my mom.

　　被動語氣的表示方法是主詞＋be動詞＋動詞第三態變化（過去分詞），例如：

I wrote the book last year.（主動）

The book was written by me last year.（被動）

　　我們很少用中文表達「被動」的觀念，我們有時說：「昨天我的眼鏡破了！」我的眼鏡其實自己不會破，是我打破的（I broke my glasses yesterday）。如果要用英語直接翻譯「昨天我的眼鏡破了！」就是：My glasses were broken yesterday. 是用被動語氣來表達。（glasses 可以是「眼鏡」的意思，也可以是「玻璃杯」的複數。）

15-1 生字

picture	圖畫
paint	畫畫，塗油漆（paint, painted, painted）
give	給（give, gave, given）
present	禮物
break	打破（break, broke, broken）
wash	洗（wash, washed, washed）
send	寄（send, sent, sent）
e-mail	電子郵件（伊媚兒）

This picture was painted by my mom. 這張圖是我媽媽畫的。
My mom painted it an hour ago. 我媽媽一小時前畫。（it代表picture）

My grandma gave me a present. 我的祖母給我一個禮物。
This toy car was given to me by her. 這輛玩具車是她給我的。

Who broke the bowls and dishes? 誰打破了這些碗盤？
My cat broke them. 我的貓打破的。（them 代表 bowls and dishes）
They were broken by my cat. 它們是被我的貓打破的。（they 代表 bowls and dishes）

Who washed the dishes? 誰洗了碗？
My brother washed them. 我哥哥洗的。
Those dishes were washed by him. 那些碗是被他洗的。

Who sent this e-mail? 誰寄的這封伊媚兒？
My uncle sent it. 我叔叔寄的。
This e-mail was sent by him. 這封伊媚兒是被他寄的。

15-2-1 圖表

現在式主動	I	write	a letter sometimes.
現在式被動	A letter	is written	by me sometimes.
過去式主動	I	wrote	a letter last night.
過去式被動	A letter	was written	by me last night.
現在完成式主動	I	have written	a letter.
現在完成式被動	A letter	has been written	by me.
過去完成式主動	I	had written	a letter before she came back.
過去完成式被動	A letter	had been written	by me before she came back.
未來式主動	I	will write	a letter this afternoon.
未來式被動	A letter	will be written	by me this afternoon.

15-3-1 選選看

1. The picture was painted _____ me. （1）of （2）by （3）at

2. My brother _____ a letter to his friend yesterday. （1）has written （2）writes （3）wrote

3. My mother gave me a present. It was _____ by my mom. （1）gave （2）given （3）give

4. The bowls were _____ by my dog. （1）break （2）broke （3）broken

5. My sister made the cake _____ hour ago. （1）an （2）a （3）two

6. The letter _____ by me. （1）has sent （2）is sending （3）was sent

7. The teacher _____ me a toy car. （1）given （2）gave （3）was given

8. My homework _____ finished by me. （1）are （2）has （3）was

9. I wrote an _____ to my friend. （1）letter （2）e-mail （3）homework

10. This book was _____ by him. （1）written （2）writing （3）wrote

11. He _____ for three hours. （1）paints （2）is painting （3）has been painting

12. These flowers _____ to me by my students. （1）was given （2）were given （3）were give

13. These pictures _____ by my students. （1）are painted （2）were paint （3）were painted

14. The work _____ by my friends this afternoon. （1）will finish （2）will finished （3）will be finished

15. Who painted the house? The house _____ by my son. （1）are painted （2）was painted （3）will be painted

15-3-2 換成被動語態說說看：

1. I made these cookies for my sisters last night.
   These cookies were made by me for my sisters last night.

2. My teacher gave me a present yesterday.

   _____

3. My father wrote this letter yesterday.

   _____

4. My brother broke the window（窗）.

   _____

5. Amy sent these e-mails to her friends.

   _____

6. I finished my homework at 8 o'clock.

   _____

7. David washed the car for his father this afternoon.

   _____

8. My sister washed the windows yesterday.

   _____

9. My brother and I cleaned the house（打掃屋子）last week.

   _____

10. My grandparents made the lunch for us yesterday.

_____

11. He painted this picture last night.

_____

12. Amy finished reading the book this afternoon.

_____

13. She wrote this novel last year.

_____

14. I often write some e-mails to my friends.

_____

15. Tom makes his bed every morning.

_____

15-3-3 英文（被動語態）該怎麼說？

1. Who will wash this dog?

   Amy 會幫狗洗澡。

   This dog _____.

2. Who broke the window（窗）？

   他的學生打破窗子的。

   The window _____.

3. Who gave the singer the flowers?

   那些學生給這位歌星花。

   The flowers _____to the singer _____.

4. Who made the bed?

   我的哥哥鋪的床。

   The bed _____.

5. Who made the cake?

   為了我的生日我的學生做蛋糕給我。

   The cake _____for my birthday.

6. Who finished his homework?

   David 寫完了功課。

   David's homework _____.

7. Who broke your glasses?

   我的眼鏡是被我的貓打破的。

   My glasses _____.

8. Who wrote this letter?

   這封信是我爸爸寫的。

   This letter _____.

9. Who drank the milk?

   我的貓喝了牛奶。

   The milk _____.

10. Who sent this e-mail?

    我的老師寄的伊媚兒。

    This e-mail _____.

11. Who painted this picture?

    我的祖父畫的這幅畫。

    This picture _____.

12. Who have played this computer game?

    我們玩過了這個電腦遊戲。

    This computer game _____.

13. Who have read this novel?

這本小說我的祖母讀過了。

This novel _____.

14. Who saw this movie last night?

這些護士(the nurses)看了這部片子。

This movie _____.

15. Who found my dog yesterday?

這位醫生(the doctor)找到了你的狗。

Your dog _____.

第十六課

現在分詞和過去分詞

（加 ing 還是加 ed?）

　　boring 和 bored（無聊）、exciting 和 excited（刺激）、interesting 和 interested（有趣）、tiring 和 tired（疲憊）以及 surprising 和 surprised（驚訝），同一組形容詞，有的結尾是 ing，有些的結尾卻是 ed。到底什麼時候用 ing？什麼時候又該用 ed 呢？我們舉 boring 和 bored 當例子來說明：

He is boring.（他是一個無聊，沒有什麼趣味的人。）

He is bored.（他覺得很無聊。）

16-1 生字

story	故事
bored	（覺得）無聊
boring	（人或事情的本身）很無聊
interested	（覺得）有趣
interesting	（人或事情的本身）很有趣
excited	（覺得）興奮、刺激
exciting	（人或事情的本身）很興奮、刺激
surprised	（覺得）驚訝
surprising	（人或事情的本身）很令人驚訝
terrible	糟糕
stupid	愚蠢、笨的
teenager	（十幾歲的）青少年
famous	有名
person	人
popular	受歡迎的
news	新聞
hear	聽到（hear, heard, heard）

16-2 課文

This story is boring.

這個故事很無聊。

I'm bored of this stupid story.

我對這個愚蠢的故事感到無聊。

I'm interested in that famous singer.

我對那位有名的歌星很感興趣。

She is an interesting person.

她是個有趣的人。

This new computer game is popular in Taiwan.

這個新的電腦遊戲在台灣很受歡迎。

Many teenagers are excited about it.

許多青少年很為它興奮。

It's very exciting to play this computer game.

玩這個電腦遊戲真令人興奮。

It was a long and tiring day today.

今天真是又長又累的一天。

I was very tired today.

我覺得今天很累。

I was surprised to hear this terrible news.

我很驚訝聽到這個可怕的新聞。

This news was surprising to me.

這個新聞對我來說真是太令人吃驚了。

16-3 because（因為）

I'm interested because it's interesting.

我覺得有趣，因為這件事太有趣了。

I'm bored because it's boring.

我覺得無聊，因為這件事很無聊。

I'm tired because it's tiring.

我覺得累，因為這件事很累人。

I'm excited because it's exciting.

我覺得興奮，因為這件事令人興奮。

I'm surprised because it's surprising.

我覺得驚訝，因為這件事令人驚訝。

 ## 16-4 介系詞後面接的動詞要加 ing

I'm tired of reading this boring novel.（be tired of 有厭煩的的意思）

我很厭煩讀這本無聊的小說。

He's interested in watching TV.

他對看電視很有興趣。

I'm excited about going to America next month.

我很興奮下個月要去美國。

She's tired of doing the dishes.

她很厭煩洗碗。

My mom is tired of cooking.

我的媽媽很厭煩做飯。

David is bored of seeing this stupid movie.

David 覺得看這部愚蠢的電影很無聊。

They are interested in reading this good novel.

他們對讀這本好小說覺得很有興趣。

＊注意：介系詞後面的動詞要加 ing 。

＊介系詞的用法各有不同，最好整個詞記下來：

　　be tired <u>of</u>

　　be interested <u>in</u>

　　be bored <u>of</u>

　　be excited <u>about</u> 接名詞

　　be surprised <u>at</u> 接名詞

　　be excited <u>to</u> 接動詞原形

　　be surprised <u>to</u> 接動詞原形

16-5-1 填填看（ing 還是 ed?）：

1. This is an _____ story. I'm _____ in it.（interest）
2. The students don't like this _____ class. They are _____ of it.（bore）
3. My mother is _____ about the good news. The news is _____.（excite）
4. My father had a _____ day. He was very _____.（tire）
5. I was _____ to see my friends in the afternoon. It was a _____ afternoon.（surprise）
6. My brother is _____ in cooking.（interest）
7. The dog is _____ to see me.（excite）
8. It's _____ to play computer games.（bore）
9. It's _____ to walk to school.（tire）
10. My grandpa was _____ at the news.（surprise）

16-5-2 選選看：

1. Many teenagers are excited _____ his new book.（1）to （2）about （3）of
2. My sister is interested _____ that famous singer.（1）in （2）on （3）at
3. I am bored _____ this story.（1）in （2）on （3）of

4. The news was surprising _____ us. (1) to (2) on (3) about
5. I am tired _____ it's a tiring day. (1) with (2) after (3) because
6. My cousin is excited _____ play the new computer game. (1) in (2) to (3) on
7. This is a _____ book. I don't want to read it. (1) boring (2) bore (3) bored
8. It was _____ to ride my new bike. (1) excited (2) excites (3) exciting
9. My mother was _____ to see my grandma. (1) surprise (2) surprised (3) surprising
10. I am _____. I don't want to go to school. (1) tiring (2) tired (3) tires

16-5-3 英文該怎麼說?

1. 在台灣她是位很受歡迎(popular)的歌星。

    _____

2. 我的媽媽對這本愚蠢的(stupid)書感到無聊。

    _____

3. Amy 寫了(has written)一本很受歡迎的小說。

    _____

4. 我的爸爸很驚訝聽到這個可怕的(terrible)消息。

    _____

5. 我很興奮要去美國。

    _____

6. 我的哥哥有個令人疲倦的(tiring)禮拜。

    _____

7.　做餅乾真有趣。It's interesting...

_____

8.　我對做菜(cooking)很有興趣。

_____

9.　David 覺得無聊因為(because)他正在讀一本無聊的書。

_____

10.　這個新聞對我們家(to my family)來說很驚人。

_____

16-5-4 改錯

1.　I was so exciting about that good news.
2.　He's interesting in painting.
3.　I was very tiring because I had a lot of homework.
4.　I'm not interested of going to school.
5.　She is bored of listen to this music many times.
6.　It's exciting to hearing that good news.
7.　I'm surprised to seeing her here.
8.　My grandma was exciting about this news.
9.　His dad is interested in do the dishes.
10.　I'm tired of make my bed every day.

第十七課

訂計畫

What are you going to do?

　　我們常常訂了許多計畫：下午要打掃房間(clean my room)、晚上讀英文(study English)、明天寄伊媚兒給朋友(send e-mails to friends)、下星期開始打籃球(play basketball)、下個月要去台北(go to Taipei)……。這些訂的計畫通常用在未來要做的事，英文用 be going to 來表示，請不要忘記，to 的後面要用動詞原形。例如：

- I'm going to see a movie tonight.

  我今晚要去看電影。

- He's going to buy a computer tomorrow.

  他明天要去買部電腦。

17-1 生字

free	自由、有空(形容詞)
be going to	計畫；打算
baseball game	棒球賽
know	知道(know, knew, known)
miss	1. 錯過 (I just missed a bus. 我剛錯過一班巴士。)
	2. 想念(I miss my friends. 我想念我的朋友。)
with	和(介系詞)
go shopping	上街購物
buy	買(buy, bought, bought)
socks	襪子(socks 通常有一雙,要加 s)
jeans	牛仔褲 (a pair of jeans 一條牛仔褲)

(注意：jeans 、 pants 褲子、 shorts 短褲都要用複數加 s 來表示)

fun	樂趣
thanks	多謝

A：Are you free tomorrow?

A：你明天有空嗎？

B：No. I'm going to watch a baseball game in Taipei.

B：沒有，我明天計畫去台北看棒球賽。

A：A baseball game? I didn't know you were interested in baseball games.

A：棒球賽？我不知道你喜歡棒球賽。

B：It will be a very exciting game. I don't want to miss it.

B：它是很刺激的球賽，我不想錯過。

A：Who will go with you?

A：誰會跟你去？

B：I will go by myself. What are you going to do tomorrow?

B：我自己獨自去。你明天計畫做什麼？

A：I'm going to go shopping.

A：我要上街買東西。

B：What are you going to buy?

B：你打算買什麼？

A：I'm going to buy some socks, T-shirts, and blue jeans.

A：我打算買一些襪子、短袖運動衫和藍色牛仔褲。

B：Have fun!

B：祝你（上街）愉快！

A：Thanks! You, too.

A：多謝，你也是。

17-3-1 圖表（肯定句）

I	am going to	buy some socks.
You	are going to	ride a bicycle to school.
He	is going to	watch an exciting basketball game on TV.
She	is going to	see an interesting movie.
We	are going to	buy some beautiful skirts（裙子）.
They	are going to	drink some coffee together.
You	are going to	call your grandparents tonight.

 17-3-2 圖表（否定句）

I	am not	going to	buy some socks.
You	are not	going to	ride a bicycle to school.
He	is not	going to	watch an exciting basketball game on TV.
She	is not	going to	see an interesting movie.
We	are not	going to	buy some beautiful skirts（裙子）.
They	are not	going to	drink some coffee together.
You	are not	going to	call your grandparents tonight.

17-3-3 圖表（問句）

Am	I going to	buy some socks?
Are	you going to	ride a bicycle to school?
Is	he going to	watch an exciting basketball game on TV?
Is	she going to	see an interesting movie?
Are	we going to	buy some beautiful skirts（裙子）？
Are	they going to	drink some coffee together?
Are	you going to	call your grandparents tonight?

17-4-1 選選看：

1. What are you going to_____ tomorrow? （1）doing （2）do （3）done

2. How much _____ your blue jeans? （1）are （2）is （3）be

3. Who _____ go with you to school? （1）is （2）has （3）will

4. What is your father going to _____? （1）buy （2）buying （3）bought

5. I don't want to _____ it. （1）missed （2）missing （3）miss

6. You _____ make a cake tomorrow. （1）have （2）are going to （3）are

7. She is going to go shopping _____. （1）together （2）by themselves （3）by herself

8. They _____ see their grandparents next week. （1）will going to （2）are going to （3）is going to

9. I _____ see a movie this evening. （1）will going to （2）am go to （3）am going to

10. A：I'm going to watch a baseball game tomorrow. B：_____! （1）How are you （2）Have fun （3）Too bad

17-4-2 問答題：（請詳答）

1. What are you going to do tomorrow?
   看朋友。_____

2. What is your sister going to do tomorrow?

看棒球賽。 _____

3. What is your mother going to do tomorrow?

買東西。 _____

4. What is your father going to do this evening?

打電話給他的父母。 _____

5. What are your cousins going to do tomorrow?

玩撲克牌。 _____

6. What is your grandma going to do tomorrow?

做餅乾。 _____

7. What are you going to do with Amy tomorrow?

一起(together)喝咖啡 _____

8. What are your teachers going to do tomorrow?

讀小說。 _____

9. What is your brother going to do this afternoon?

做功課。 _____

10. What is David going to do in the afternoon?

睡午覺。 _____

17-4-3 看圖回答問題：

What is Amy going to buy tomorrow?

1. She's going to buy some socks.

2. _____
_____
_____

3. _____
_____

4. _____
_____

5. _____
_____

6. _____
_____

7. _____
_____

8. _____
_____

9. _____
_____

10. _____
_____

17-4-4 改錯：

1. She will going to read a novel.
2. My dad is going to eating pork.
3. Are you going buy some eggs?
4. I will not going to buy a computer.
5. He does not going to meet his friends tonight.
6. My parents is not going to see that movie.
7. We will going to see you tomorrow.
8. How many times is you going to meet her?
9. You are going see that movie with her.
10. I'm going to reading that interesting novel tonight.

第十八課

多久一次

How often...?

我們常問別人「多久上街買一次東西？」、「多久看一次小說？」、「多久游一次泳？」、「多久去一趟台北」？

「多久」用英文來表達就是 how often。例如：

· How often do you go shopping? 你多久上街買一次東西？

· How often do you read novels? 你多久看一次小說？

· How often do you go swimming? 你多久游一次泳？

· How often do you go to Taipei? 你多久去一趟台北？

這些問題有很多種答案：「一星期一次」、「兩個月一次」、「一年三次」……。有時我們也可以用 sometimes（有時），often（常常），seldom（很少），hardly ever（幾乎不）來回答。

How often...是問一個人的習慣，所以通常會用現在式來表達。

18-1 生字

once	一次
twice	兩次
time	次數

(＊注意：一次 once ，兩次 twice ，三次以上用 times)

once in a while	有時(sometimes)
department store	百貨公司
museum	博物館

(art museum 美術館， science museum 科學博物館)

walk	走路（take a walk 散步）
walk the dog	遛狗
go swimming	游泳
go jogging	慢跑
exercise	運動(在本課當動詞)
sport	運動(名詞)
kind	種類
no wonder	怪不得
look	看起來
busy	忙

18-2 課文

A：How often do you go shopping?

A：你多久上街買一次東西？

B：I go to the department store once a week.

B：我一星期去一次百貨公司。

A：How often do you and your sister go to the museum?

A：你和你的姊姊多久去一次博物館？

B：We go there twice a month.

B：我們一個月去兩次。

A：How often does Amy walk the dog?

A：Amy 多久遛一次狗？

B：She walks the dog every day.

B：她每天都遛狗。

A：How often do your parents exercise?

A：你的父母多久運動一次？

B：They exercise three times a week.

B：他們一星期運動 3 次。

A：What kind of sports do they do?

A：他們做哪一種運動？

B：My mom goes swimming, and my dad goes jogging.

B：我的媽媽去游泳，我的爸爸慢跑。

A：No wonder they look so healthy.

A：怪不得他們看起來這麼的健康。

B：How often do you exercise?

B：你多久運動一次？

A：I seldom exercise because I'm too busy.

A：我很少運動，因為我太忙了。

 18-3 圖表

How often	do	you	go shopping?
I	go shopping		once a day.
How often	does	he	go jogging?
He	goes jogging		four times a week.
How often	does	she	go swimming?
She	goes swimming		twice a week.
How often	do	you	see your grandparents?
We	see	them	three times a year.
How often	do	they	read comic books?
They	hardly ever	read	comic books.

18-4-1 填填看：

1. My father _____ every day. （遛狗）
2. My grandfather goes to the park _____. （有時）
3. Your friend came to see you; _____ you looked happy yesterday. （怪不得）
4. We go to America _____. （一年兩次）
5. My brother _____ in the morning. （慢跑）
6. _____ do you exercise? （多久一次）
7. What _____ sports does your sister do? （種類）
8. My mother goes shopping _____. （一星期 3 次）
9. I see Amy _____. （一個月兩次）
10. He seldom exercises because he is _____. （太忙）
11. She hardly ever goes to the _____. （美術館）
12. They seldom go to the _____. （科學館）
13. I'm _____ in sports. （沒興趣）
14. His children enjoy _____ to the museum. （去）
15. My father is _____ of walking the dog every day. （厭煩）

18-4-2 請根據自己的情況回答下列問題：（請詳答）

1. How often do you go to the museum?

   _____

2.　How often do you go shopping?

_____

3.　How often do you buy milk?

_____

4.　How often do you listen to music?

_____

5.　How often does your father do the dishes?

_____

6.　How often do you read novels?

_____

7.　How often do you exercise?

_____

8.　How often do you brush your teeth?

_____

9.　How often do you go swimming?

_____

10.　How often do you see movies?

_____

18-4-3 英文該怎麼說？

1.　David 一個月去博物館 3 次。

_____

2.　我的爸爸一星期去百貨公司兩次。

_____

3.　我一星期游 3 次泳。

_____

4.　我的姊姊很少(seldom)燒飯(cook)因為她太忙了。

_____

5.　他每天運動；怪不得他看起來這麼(so)健康。

_____

6.　我的貓有時打破碗(break bowls)。

_____

7.　我每天在公園裡遛狗。

_____

8.　你多久運動(exercise)一次？

_____

9.　我的小孩(children)每天刷牙兩次。

_____

10.　我的英文老師每星期去學校 5 次。

_____

11.　我的祖父每星期在公園裡散步(take a walk)3 次。

_____

12.　她的祖父母一年去一次日本。

_____

13.　他的弟弟覺得每天遛狗很無聊。

_____

14.　她對運動(sports)很感興趣。

_____

15.　Amy 幾乎不運動。

_____

第十九課

必須做的事情

You must...

You must take a shower.

　　我們常聽人問：「你現在必須做功課」、「你應該回家了」、「你最好不要玩電玩了」、「你一定累壞了」。這些「必須」(have to)、「應該」(should)、「最好」(had better)、「一定」(must)口氣雖略有不同，不過相同的是：這些詞的後面都必須接動詞原形。

19-1 生字

must	一定，必須
have to	必須 (比 must 口氣緩和些)
had better	最好 (had 一定要用過去式)
should	應該
take a rest	休息
think	想 (think, thought, thought)
wait a minute	等一等
teddy bear	泰迪熊 (以熊為造型的填充玩偶)
cute	可愛
really	真的 (not really 不見得)
cost	值
expensive	貴 (相反詞是 cheap 便宜)
taxi	計程車
safe	安全

19-2 課文

A：You must be tired.

A：你一定是累壞了。

B：Yes, I am. I worked twelve hours today.

B：我是很累。我今天工作了 12 個小時。

A：You had better take a rest.

A： 你最好休息一下。

B：It's late. I think I should go home now.

B： 很晚了。我想我現在應該回家。

A：Wait a minute. You must see this before you go.

A：等一等。你回家以前一定得看這個。

B：What's that?

B： 那是什麼？

A：It's a teddy bear. I bought it at the department store.

A：它是泰迪熊。我在百貨公司買的。

B：It's very cute. It must be very expensive.

B：它很可愛。它一定很貴吧。

A：Not really. It only costs two hundred NT dollars.

A：不見得。它只值台幣 200 元。

B：O.K. I have to go now. Should I take a taxi or a bus?

B：好，我現在必須走了。我應該搭計程車還是搭巴士？

A：You had better take a bus because it's safer.

A：你最好搭巴士，因為比較安全。

19-3-1 must (必須,一定)/ mustn't (不行)

· This book must be good.

　這本書一定很棒。

· You must take a shower tonight.

　今晚你必須洗澡。

· You must not (mustn't) play computer games now.

　你現在不能玩電腦遊戲了。

 19-3-2 have to(必須)比 must 口語化,也較 must 常用

· I have to call my mom tonight.

　今晚我必須打電話給媽媽。

· I don't have to go to school tomorrow.

　我明天不必上學。

· She doesn't have to go with me.

　她明天不必跟我去。

· Do you have to work on Saturday?

　你星期六要上班嗎?

· I had to finish my homework last night.

　我昨晚必須寫完功課。

 19-3-3 should(應該)

· I should do the dishes every day.

我應該每天洗碗。

· He should exercise every day.

他應該每天運動。

· Should I buy this expensive teddy bear?

我應該買這個昂貴的泰迪熊嗎？

· I don't think you should buy it.

我覺得你不應該買。

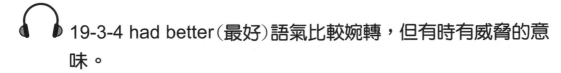 19-3-4 had better（最好）語氣比較婉轉，但有時有威脅的意味。

· I had better take a rest now.（had better 後面接動詞原形）

你現在最好休息了。

· You had better not buy that expensive purple T-shirt.

你最好不要買那件昂貴的紫色 T-shirt。

· You had better do your homework right now!

你最好現在寫功課。

19-4-1 選選看

1.   This book _____ three hundred NT dollars.（1）cost（2）costs（3）buys

2.   My brother bought the bike _____ a department store.（1）on（2）at（3）to

3.   My father didn't _____ a rest this afternoon.（1）take（2）give（3）sleep

4.   I have to _____ to school now.（1）go（2）going（3）gone

5.   It _____ be a good movie.（1）had（2）have better（3）must

6.   My cousins had better _____ their homework.（1）did（2）do（3）to do

7.   I _____ cook for my grandma.（1）should（2）have（3）has better

8.   My grandparents will _____ to my house.（1）ride a taxi（2）sit a taxi（3）take a taxi

9.   _____ I buy some apples or some oranges?（1）Have（2）Should（3）Won't

10.   You _____ go to see a doctor today.（1）had better（2）has better（3）not better

19-4-2 填填看

1.   A：I'm going to play basketball now.

      B：_____. Did you do your homework?（等一下）

2. A：He must be very sad.

   B：_____. He is happy today.（不見得）

3. A：This teddy bear is very _____. Where did you buy it?（可愛）

   B：I bought it _____ a department store.（在）

4. A：My sister worked ten hours today.

   B：She _____ be tired.（一定）

   A：Yes. She should _____.（休息）

5. A：You _____ do the dishes before Dad comes home.（最好）

   B：Yes, I think I_____ do the dishes now.（應該）

6. A：I _____ go home now.（必須）

   B：You had better take a bus because it is _____.（比較安全）

19-4-3 英文該怎麼說？

1. 我應該買這條(this pair of)貴的牛仔褲嗎？

   _____

2. 這位老師搭計程車去學校了。

   _____

3. 我必須(have to)今晚打電話給我的祖父母。

   _____

4. 你不能(mustn't)現在看電視。

   _____

5. 你的爸爸最好每星期運動 3 次。

   _____

6.   你的姊妹看起來(look)很可愛。

_____

7.   我想我應該現在鋪床。

_____

8.   晚上搭計程車安全嗎？ Is it safe...

_____

9.   我每天必須(have to)刷牙 3 次。

_____

10.   我的媽媽今天下午一定得休息(take a rest)。

_____

19-4-4 改錯：

1.   He must to do his homework now.
2.   I had better not to go to school today.
3.   Amy must to take a bus to school.
4.   Do I had to take a shower before I watch TV?
5.   My children must to make their beds every day.
6.   Should I to buy this expensive table?
7.   She shouldn't call her teacher at Sunday night.
8.   My grandma had better to take a nap because she looks very tired.
9.   Does she has to do the dishes tonight?
10.   I think you should buy that pair of jeans because it is cheap.

第二十課

請 求

May I...?

Do you mind...?

Excuse me. May I borrow your bike?

我們常聽小孩說我要這個，我要那個，I want this...I want that...，其實不論是用英文或中文，這樣的口氣都顯得很霸道、沒有禮貌。比較合適的說法是 May I...或是 Do you mind...?

20-1 生字

excuse me	對不起（引人注意時用語）
May I...?	我可以……嗎？
borrow...from	向某人借（borrow, borrowed, borrowed）
lend...to	借出給某人 (lend, lent, lent)
sorry	對不起（道歉時用語）
in a minute	一分鐘之內（指短時間內，馬上）
Do you mind...?	你介不介意……？（如果不介意，回答要用 No, I don't.）
a few	一些（用於可數的名詞前，如：a few apples）
a little	一些（用於不可數的名詞前，如：a little time）
not at all	一點也不
look at	注視，看著某人或某個東西
take a look	看一下
sure	毫無疑問的，確定的
go ahead	看吧，拿吧，用吧，去吧。
take a picture	照一張照片（picture 是圖畫也可以是照片）
wonderful	好棒
thank you	謝謝你

A : Excuse me. May I borrow your bike?

A : 對不起，我可以借你的腳踏車嗎？（bike 是 bicycle 的簡稱）

B : I'm sorry; I just lent it to my brother.

B : 很抱歉；我剛剛把它借給我的哥哥了。

A : When will he come back?

A : 他什麼時候回來？

B : He will be home in a minute.

B : 他一會兒就會回家了。

A : Do you mind if I borrow it for a few days?

A : 你介意如果我借你的腳踏車借幾天嗎？

B : No, not at all.

B : 不，一點都不介意。

A : What are you looking at?

A : 你正在看什麼？

B : Some pictures.

B : 一些照片。

A：May I take a look?

A：我可以看一下嗎？

B：Sure, go ahead. I took these pictures at Kenting.

B：好，去看吧。我在墾丁照的這些相片。

A：You look wonderful in the pictures.

A：你在照片中看起來好棒。

B：Thank you.

B：謝謝你。

🎧 20-2-1 May I...?和 Could I...? 意思相同

1. May I borrow this book from you?

   我可以跟你借這本書嗎？

   Sure, go ahead.

   當然，拿去吧。

2. Could I use your telephone?

   我可以用你的電話嗎？

   Sure, go ahead.

   當然，去用吧。

3. Do you mind if I borrow your car?

   你介意如果我跟你借車嗎？

   I'm sorry; I can't lend it to you. I have to use it tomorrow.

   對不起，我不能借給你。我明天得用它。

20-3-1 填填看

1.　A：Excuse me. May I _____ your chair?（借）

　　B：_____. I will use it in a minute.（對不起）

2.　A：Do you _____ if I eat your cookies?（介意）

　　B：No, _____.（一點也不）

3.　A：May I _____ at the pictures?（看一下）

　　B：_____.（看吧）

4.　A：My sister looks _____ in the picture.（很棒）

　　B：Yes. You look beautiful, too.

5.　A：Could you _____ of Amy and me?（照相）

　　B：Wait a minute（等一下）. I will be back in a minute.

6.　A：I don't have any money.

　　B：Ask your father to _____ you some money.（借給）

7.　A：Is your mother here?

　　B：No. She will be home _____.（一分鐘之內）

20-3-2 用 lend 還是 borrow?

1.　May I _____ your pencil? (lend, borrow)

2.　Amy _____ me some money. (lent, borrowed)

3.　Tom _____ a book from me last night.（lent, borrowed）

4.　Who _____ our basketball? (lent, borrowed)

5. Could you _____ your car to me? (lend, borrow)

6. I never _____ money from my friends. (lend, borrow)

7. She will _____ me her Teddy Bear. (lend, borrow)

8. I don't like to _____ her my bike. (lend, borrow)

9. He doesn't want to _____ his computer to me. (lend, borrow)

10. She won't _____ money from her mom. (lend, borrow)

20-3-3 改錯

1. May I lend your bike?

2. What are you looking in?

3. May I took a look?

4. You look wonderful at the pictures.

5. Do you mind if I lend your car for a few days?

6. I just borrowed a novel to my friend.

7. May I to use your telephone?

8. My mother takes those pictures in America.

9. I borrow this pencil from Amy yesterday.

10. My sister is going to Taipei in few days.

20-3-4 想一想再回答：

1. Do you mind if there are no flowers in your room?

2. Do you mind if there are no pictures in your room?

3. Do you mind singing in the classroom?

4. Do you mind doing your homework every day?

5. Do you mind going to bed late every day?

6. Do you mind playing the piano for your friends?

7. Do you mind doing the dishes every day?

8. Do you mind if the music is loud（大聲）?

9. Do you mind if you cannot play computer games?

10. Do you mind lending money to your friends?（借錢給朋友）

第二十一課

建議

Let's...

　　朋友聚在一起的時候，常有人提議一起去打球，或一起去看一場電影。這些建議可以用 let's 來表達。例如：

Let's play basketball now.（我們現在去打籃球吧！）

Let's go to see a movie now.（我們現在去看一場電影吧！）

let's 是 let us...（讓我們……）的縮寫。除了「讓我們」(let us)之外，我們也常常說：

‧ Let me do it. 讓我來做吧！

‧ I'll let you do it. 讓你來做吧！

‧ Let her do it. 讓她來做吧！

‧ Let him do it. 讓他來做吧！

‧ Let them do it. 讓他們來做吧！

‧ I'll let you do it. 讓你們來做吧！

＊注意：let...後面要接動詞原形。

21-1 生字

write	寫（write, wrote, written）
see	看（see, saw, seen）
about	關於（介系詞）
pet	寵物
know	知道（know, knew, known）
rabbit	兔子
later	待會兒
first	先
food	食物

A：What are you going to write for your homework?

A：你的家庭作業打算寫什麼？

B：Let me see. I think I will write about my pets.

B：讓我想看看。我想我會寫關於我的寵物的事情。（let me see 有讓我想想看的意思。）

A：I didn't know you have pets.

A：我不知道你有寵物。

B：I have two birds and one rabbit.

B：我有兩隻鳥和一隻兔子。

A：Let's go to your house to take a look at your pets.

A：我們去你家看一看你的寵物。

B：Let them sleep for a while. We can go later.

B：讓牠們睡一會兒，我們待會兒再去。

A：What should we do now?

A：我們現在該做什麼呢？

B：Let's go shopping first.

B：我們先去逛街。

A：What are you going to buy?

A：你打算買什麼？

B：We can buy some pet food for my birds and my rabbit.

B：我們可以買一些寵物食物給我的鳥和兔子。

21-2-1 Let ＋人稱代名詞受格

· Let me read the novel first. We can go later.

讓我先讀小說，我們可以待會兒再去。

· Let him watch TV first. We can talk to him later.

讓他先看電視，我們可以待會兒再和他說。

· Let her call her mom first. We can meet her later.

讓她先打電話給她媽媽，我們可以待會兒再跟她見面。

· Let it eat its pet food first. We can play with it later.

讓牠先吃牠的寵物食物，我們待會兒再跟牠玩。

· Let's play computer games first. We can do the dishes later.

讓我們先玩電腦遊戲，我們可以待會兒再洗碗。

· I'll let you finish your homework first. I can call you later.

讓你們先做功課，我待會兒再打電話給你們。

· Let them go jogging first. We can go shopping with them later.

讓他們先慢跑，我們待會兒再跟他們去逛街買東西。

21-3-1 選選看

1.　A：What should we do now?

　　B：＿＿＿＿＿＿＿ go to the park first.

　　(1) Let them　(2) Let's　(3) Let me

2.　A：What are you going to write to your father?

　　B：I think I will write ＿＿＿＿＿＿＿ my school.

　　(1) about　(2) for　(3) to

3.　A：I'm going to Taipei to see my girlfriend.

　　B：I ＿＿＿＿＿＿＿ know you have a girlfriend.

　　(1) won't　(2) wouldn't　(3) didn't

4.　A：Do you want to ＿＿＿＿＿＿＿ at my new house?

　　B：Of course.（當然）

　　(1) take look　(2) take a look　(3) take looks

5.　A：Can we go shopping now?

　　B：＿＿＿＿＿＿＿ me read this novel first. We can go later.

　　(1) Let's　(2) She lets　(3) Let

6.　A：Let him ＿＿＿＿＿＿＿ the dishes.

　　B：He may break the dishes.

　　(1) do　(2) to do　(3) doing

7.　A：Let's ＿＿＿＿＿＿＿ to see a movie now.

　　B：I'm sorry. I don't have time.

(1)going　(2)don't go　(3)go

8.　A：What _____ do now?

B：Let's play basketball.

(1)are we　(2)should we　(3)must we to

9.　A：What are we going to buy?

B：We can buy _____ pet food.

(1)a few　(2)some　(3)many

10.　A：May I borrow some money from you?

B：Sorry, I don't have _____.

(1)much　(2)many　(3)some

21-3-2 英文該怎麼說？

1.　讓他先睡個午覺。

_____

2.　讓她先(first)看電視；她可以等會兒(later)再洗碗。

_____

3.　讓這位學生先說(talk)；我們待會兒再說。

_____

4.　我讓她先走。

_____

5.　我媽媽總是(always)讓我先洗澡。

_____

6.　我們明天去台北。 Let's...

_____

7.　讓我看看(take a look at)你的功課。

_____

8. 我可以玩一下（for a while）電腦遊戲嗎？

_____

9. 我們現在該（should）做什麼？

_____

10. 你幫你的兔子買了寵物食物了嗎？ Did you...

_____

21-3-3 改錯

1. Let her goes to school first. We can talk to her later.
2. I let my brother does the homework for me.
3. She lets me reads her novel.
4. Tom always lets me driving his car.
5. My sister won't let me to ride her bike.
6. Let's go. We didn't have much time.
7. Let's to play computer games this afternoon.
8. Let them doing the dishes.
9. Let me to see your pictures.
10. She is look wonderful in the pictures.

第二十二課

找東西

Where is...?

Where is my knife?

東西找不到時最讓人煩惱,你若大聲問:"Where is my hat?"(我的帽子在哪裡?),一定有人邊問邊幫你找:

· Is it in your bag?(它在你的袋子裡嗎?)

· Is it on the table?(它在桌上嗎?)

· Is it under your chair?(它在椅子下面嗎?)

22-1 生字

watch	手表
leave	留在，離開 (leave, left, left)
tea table	茶几
living room	客廳
maybe	也許，或許
bookshelf	書架 (bookshelf 的複數是 bookshelves)
bedroom	卧房
either	用於否定
put	放 (put, put, put)
under	……的下面
next to	……的旁邊
disappear	不見，失蹤
in front of	……的前面
eyes	眼睛

A：Mom, where is my watch?

A：媽，我的手表在哪裡？

B：You left it on the tea table in the living room.

B：你把它留在客廳茶几上。

A：I can't find it.

A：我找不到啊。

B：Maybe it's on the bookshelf in your bedroom.

B：也許在你房間書架上。

A：It's not there, either.

A：也沒有在那裡。

B：Then, I don't know where you put it.

B：那麼，我不知道你放在哪裡了。

A：Mom, I have found it. It's under my desk.

A：媽，我找到了，它在我的桌子底下。

B：See, I always put my watch on the table next to the bed.

B：看，我總是把我的手表放在床旁邊的桌子上。（see 是 you see 的簡寫）

A：O.K. I will put it on my desk, so it won't disappear in front of my eyes.

A：好吧，我會把它放在我的書桌上，那麼，它就不會從我眼前消失了。

22-2-1 表示地點的用詞

on the desk 在書桌上
under the desk 在書桌下
in front of the desk 在書桌前
behind the desk 在書桌後
in the desk 在書桌裡面（在抽屜裡）
next to the desk 在書桌旁邊

22-2-2 maybe 和 may 意思相同，但是 maybe 後面不能加動詞，而 may 後面可以加動詞原形。

（✗）He maybe call me tonight.
（○）Maybe he will call me tonight.
（○）He may call me tonight.

 22-2-3 I don't know...

注意：由問句變成敘述句時，主詞動詞要調換位置。

A：Where is he?　　　　　　B：I don't know where he is.
A：How old is your mom?　　B：I don't know how old she is.
A：When is her birthday?　　B：I don't know when her birthday is.
A：What is this?　　　　　　B：I don't know what this is.

22-3-1 由直接問句變為敘述句。

1.　Where is your brother?　I don't know where he_____.

2.　When is Amy's birthday?　I don't know when her birthday_____.

3.　Where are your sister's socks?　I don't know where they _____.

4.　How is your grandfather?　I don't know how he _____.

5.　What is his name?　I don't know what his name_____.

6.　Where are my books?　I don't know where they _____.

7.　How are your aunt's cats?　I don't know how they _____.

8.　When are your friends coming here? I don't know when they _____coming.

9.　What is this?　I don't know what this _____.

10.　How is the cake?（蛋糕的味道如何？）I don't know how it _____.

22-3-2 填填看

1.　A：Where is my cup of tea?（我的那杯茶在哪裡？）

　　B：It is _____ the tea table _____ the living room.

2.　A：Where are my socks?

　　B：You left them _____ your sister's room.

3.　A：Where is the movie theater?

　　B：I'm sorry.　I don't know.

　　C：I don't know, _____ .（也）

4.　A：Where is your bag?

　　B：I always put it _____ （旁邊）my desk.

5.　A：Where is David?

　　B：He is standing _____ （前面）Amy.

6.　A：Where are your dogs?

　　B：They are _____ the tree（在樹下）.

7.　A：Where is my hat?

　　B：It's _____ the door.（在門後面）

8.　A：Where is my cell phone?

　　B：I don't know where you put _____ .

9.　A：Where are my glasses?

　　B：I don't know. They won't _____ .（消失）

10.　A：Where are my jeans?

　　B：See, _____ are on your bed.

22-3-3 英文該如何說？

1.　我的祖母找不到（find）她的眼鏡。

　　_____

2.　這隻兔子在我眼前消失了（disappeared）。

　　_____

3.　報紙在茶几下面。 The newspaper...

　　_____

4.　也許你的襯衫在我的臥房。 Maybe...

　　_____

5.　我也（either）看不到這隻鳥。

　　_____

6. 我的手表在哪裡？

　　　_____

7. 我哥哥有 3 個書架(bookshelves)在他的卧房裡。

　　　_____

8. 我的狗喜歡坐在我的旁邊。

　　　_____

9. 請把蛋糕放在桌上。

　　　_____

10. 我不知道你把碗放在哪裡了。

　　　_____

第二十三課

問 路

Where is...?

Excuse me, could you tell me where the ladies' room is?

　　問路是許多出外旅行的人共有的經驗，如果知道如何用英文問路，也聽得懂當地人指出的方向，一定可以節省不少時間和精力。開口問路先得說：Excuse me.（對不起）來引起對方的注意。接著可以用直接問法：Where is the art museum?（美術館在哪裡？），或者用比較婉轉的問法：Could you tell me where the art museum is?（你可以告訴我美術館在哪裡？）

23-1 生字

excuse	藉口（excuse me 抱歉）
tell	告訴（tell, told, told）
the ladies' room	女廁所
the men's room	男廁所
pardon	原諒（Pardon me. 請再說一遍）
straight	直，直接
turn	轉彎，翻轉（turn, turned, turned）
post office	郵局
right	右（turn right 右轉）
left	左（turn left 左轉）
repeat	重複（repeat, repeated, repeated）
again	再
see	看（see, saw, seen）
still	還是
take	帶（take, took, taken）
welcome	歡迎（You're welcome. 不用客氣。）

23-2 課文

A：Excuse me, could you tell me where the ladies' room is?

A：對不起，你可以告訴我女廁在哪裡嗎？

B：Pardon me?

B：請再說一遍。(沒有聽清楚。)

A：Where is the ladies' room?

A：女廁在哪裡？

B：Oh, let me see. Go straight and then turn right at the post office.

B：哦，讓我想想看。直走，然後在郵局右轉。

A：I'm sorry. Could you repeat it again?

A：很抱歉，你可以再重複一遍嗎？

B：Go straight, turn right, and the ladies' room is across from class-room 101.

B：直走，右轉，女廁在 101 教室的對面。

A：I'm sorry. I still don't know.

A：抱歉，我還是不知道。

B：Don't worry. I will take you there.

B：別擔心，我帶你去。

A：Thank you very much.

A：多謝。

B：You're welcome.

B：不客氣。

23-2-1 指示方向的詞

go straight 直走
turn right 右轉
turn left 左轉
on your right 你的右邊
on your left 你的左邊
across from you 你的對面
next to you 你的旁邊

 23-2-2 Could you tell me...

注意：組合兩個問句時，第二個問句主詞和動詞要互相調換位置。

· What is your name?（你叫什麼名字？）

→ Could you tell me what your name is?（你可以告訴我你叫什麼名字嗎？）

· Where is the art museum?（美術館在哪裡？）

→ Could you tell me where the art museum is?（你可以告訴我美術館在哪裡嗎？）

· When are you going to finish your homework?（你什麼時候會寫完功課？）

→Could you tell me when you are going to finish your homework?（你可以告訴我你什麼時候會寫完功課嗎？）

· How is your mom?（令堂如何？）

→ Could you tell me how your mom is?（你可以告訴我令堂如何嗎？）

23-3-1 填填看

1.　A：Thank you very much.

　　B：You are _____. （不用客氣）

2.　A：Could you tell me where the ladies' room is?

　　B：I'm sorry. Could you _____ it again?（重複）

3.　A：_____. Could you tell me where the school is?（對不起）

　　B：Oh, let me _____. Go straight.（我想想看）

4.　A：My name is Miranda.

　　B：_____ me?（請再說一遍）

　　A：My name is Miranda.

5.　A：Where is the bus stop?

　　B：Go straight and _____ left.（左轉）The bus stop is on your right.

6.　A：Go straight then turn right.

　　B：I'm sorry. I _____ don't know.（還是）

7.　A：Where is the department store?

　　B：It's _____ from the post office?（對面）

8.　A：Where is the science museum?（科學館）

　　B：It's _____（隔壁）to the art museum.

9.　A：Where is the men's room?

B：Let me _____.（想想看）

10. A：I'm sorry. I still don't know.

B：_____（別擔心）. I'll take you there.

23-3-2 中文該怎麼說？

1. Where is the department store?

別擔心，我媽媽會帶我們去。

_____ My mom will take us there.

2. Excuse me, could you tell me where the supermarket is?

對不起，我不知道它在哪裡。

Sorry, I don't know where_____.

3. Pardon me.

別擔心。我會再重複。

Don't _____. I will _____ it again.

4. Where is your school?

我的學校在郵局的隔壁。

My school is _____.

5. Where is the department store?

直走，再左轉。

Go straight, _____.

6. Where is the science museum?

直走，它在你的右邊。

Go straight. It is _____.

7. Thank you very much.

不要客氣。

_____

8. Where is your mom?

她在郵局裡。

She is _____.

9. What are you going to buy?

讓我想想看。

_____

10. Where is the park?

它在百貨公司的對面。

It is _____ the department store.

23-3-3 改錯

1. My mom went to department store.

2. Go straight and then turn left in the school.

3. The science museum is at your right.

4. Could you tell me where is my pencil?

5. I don't know where is the ladies' room.

6. I don't know when will he come.

7. Could you tell me who is he?

8. The art museum is next to park.

9. I saw a house is across from my school.

10. Where are you come from?

第二十四課

問時間

What time is it?

What time is it now?

我們生活中的點點滴滴都與時間有關。例如：

‧手表停了的時候問別人「現在幾點？」(What time is it?)

‧出外旅行時，需要查問車班的時刻表：「下班車幾點開？」
(What time does the next bus leave?)

‧想要看電影時，我們會問：「下一場電影是幾點？」(What time
is the next show?)

24-1 生字

be interested in	對……有興趣
with	和（介系詞）
the next	下一個
show	電影（場次）
check	查（check, checked, checked）
start	開始（start, started, started）
about	大約，關於（介系詞）
hour	小時
leave	離開（leave, left, left）
buy	買（buy, bought, bought）
newspaper	報紙
minute	分
hurry up	趕快
in	（多少時間）之內（介系詞）

A：What time is it now?

A：現在幾點？

B：It's seven twenty-five.

B：7:25。

A：Are you interested in seeing a movie with me?

A：你有興趣和我去看一場電影嗎？

(＊注意：介系詞後面的動詞要改為動名詞 see[動詞]→seeing[動名詞])

B：Which one?

B：哪一部片子？

A：That one about the baseball games.

A：那一部關於棒球賽的。

B：What time does the next show start?

B：下一場幾點開始？

A：Let me check. It starts at eight twenty.

A：讓我查查看。8:20 開始。

B：We only have about an hour.

B：我們只有差不多一小時的時間。

A：What time does the next bus leave?

A：下一班巴士幾點開？

B：Let me see. It leaves at seven forty.

B：我看看。它 7:40 離開。

A：Do I have time to buy today's newspaper?

A：我有時間買今天的報紙嗎？

B：You only have five minutes. Hurry up!

B：你只有 5 分鐘可以買。趕快！

24-2-1 時間表的問法：What time is...? / What time does...?

What time	is	the movie?電影	
What time	does	the movie	start?開始
What time	is	the bus?巴士	
What time	does	the bus	leave?離開
What time	is	the train?火車	
What time	does	the train	leave?離開
What time	is	the flight?飛機航班	
What time	does	the flight	depart?起飛

24-2-2 interest（讓某人覺得有趣）/ be interested in（有興趣）/ be interesting（有趣）

This novel is interesting. 這本小說很有趣。
This novel interests him. 這本小說讓他覺得有趣。
He is interested in this novel. 他對這本小說很有興趣。

Learning English is interesting. 學習英文很有趣。
Learning English interests him. 學習英文讓他覺得有趣。
He is interested in learning English. 他有興趣學英文。

Talking to her is interesting. 跟她說話很有趣。

Talking to her interests him. 跟她說話讓他覺得有趣。

He is interested in talking to her. 他很有興趣跟她說話。

 24-2-3　Do I have time...?

Do I have time to brush my teeth?

我有時間刷牙嗎？

Do you have time to finish your homework?

你有時間做完你的功課嗎？

Does he have time to go to the men's room?

他有時間去男廁嗎？

Does she have time to wash her hair?

她有時間洗她的頭髮嗎？

Do we have time to do the dishes?

我們有時間洗碗嗎？

Do they have time to make the beds?

他們有時間鋪床嗎？

24-3-1 選選看

1. I will be home _____ 6：45 （1）at （2）in （3）on

2. I will be home _____ 30 minutes. （1）at （2）in （3）on

3. I'm _____ in swimming. （1）interest （2）interesting （3）interested

4. Ms. Wen's English class is _____. （1）bore （2）boring （3）bored（無聊）

5. Ms. Lin's Japanese class is _____. （1）interest （2）interesting （3）interested

6. Do I have time to _____ to the ladies' room? （1）goes （2）going （3）go

7. The train leaves _____ 4:40 P.M. （1）on （2）in （3）at

8. I will meet you _____ 10:30 A.M.in front of the museum. （1）at about （2）on （3）in

9. I will go shopping with my mom _____ 3 o'clock in the afternoon. （1）for （2）at （3）in

10. This novel is _____ a girl's dream（夢）. （1）at （2）for （3）about

24-3-2 填填看

1. A：_____ now?（幾點鐘？）
   B：It is seven thirty.

2. A：Are you _____ seeing a movie with me?（有興趣）

　　B：Yes, of course.（當然）

3. A：What time does the next show start?

　　B：_____. It starts at eight twenty.（讓我查查看）

　　A：So we only have _____ an hour.（大約）

4. A：When does the next bus _____?（離開）

　　B：It leaves _____ ten fifteen.

5. A：I don't have time to buy today's _____.（報紙）

　　B：No, you don't. _____!（趕快）

24-3-3 英文該如何說？

1. 下班巴士 6 點 10 分開。

　　_____

2. 你必須一個星期內讀完這本小說。 You have to finish reading...

　　_____

3. 你有興趣跟我去看電影嗎？

　　_____

4. 下班巴士什麼時候離開？(leave)

　　_____

5. 你買了今天的報紙嗎？ Have you...

　　_____

6. 下場電影幾點開始？ What time...

　　_____

7. 電影 7:30 開始。 The movie...

　　_____

8. 現在幾點鐘？

9.　我來查查今天的報紙。

10.　你要看哪一部電影？Which movie...

24-3-4 改錯

1.　What time is the movie start?

2.　I must to go in ten minutes.

3.　Have you readed today's newspaper?

4.　The next show is start at 9:30.

5.　She's not interesting in swimming.

6.　Talk to her is very boring.

7.　I'm not interested in play computer games.

8.　You must to finish reading the newspaper in two minutes.

9.　What time is the bus leave?

10.　I don't know when does the movie start.

附錄

在《專門為中國人寫的英文課本》中級本的每一課中，我們都會介紹一個文法觀念或日常會話的常用句型，課文通常以短句或兩人對話的方式呈現。讀者學會每一課之後，可以參考附錄的範文，研究各種時態和文法規則如何在一篇文章中靈活運用。讀者讀過範文後，應該可以明瞭，即使只是一篇十來句的短文，因為句子所敘述事情的時間與口氣不同，時態也必須不斷的調整，不能只單用一種時態（如現在式）。希望大家讀完附錄的三篇範文後，更能對本書所介紹的文法觀念有一個通盤的瞭解與認識。

範文一

生字

China	中國
summer	夏天（spring 春天、 fall 秋天、 winter 冬天）
excite	令人興奮、刺激（動詞）
about	關於（介系詞）
trip	旅行（名詞，通常行程比較短，例如：take a trip to Japan）
write	寫（write, wrote, written）
Chinese	中國人、中國的
writer	作家
interest	讓人感興趣、興趣（動詞、名詞）
bore	令人無聊、無聊的人或事情（動詞、名詞）
travel	旅行（動詞、名詞）
how often	多久

Tom is going to China this summer.[1] He has never been to China.[2] He must be very excited.[3] Last night Mary was reading a novel when Tom told her about the trip.[4] The novel was written by a Chinese writer.[5] Mary is very interested in reading novels.[6] Tom is bored with reading.[7] He likes to travel.[8] How often does Mary read novels?[9] She reads novels once a week.[10]

翻譯

　　Tom今年夏天計畫去中國，他從沒去過中國，他非常興奮。昨晚當 Tom 告訴 Mary 這趟旅行時，她正在讀一本小說。這本小說是一位中國的作家寫的。Mary 很喜歡讀小說，Tom 覺得閱讀很無聊，他喜歡旅行。Mary 多久讀一次小說呢？她一星期讀一次小說。

課文解析

1.　在第十七課「訂計畫」裡，我們談到 be going to 的用法。例如：

　　· What is Tom going to do this summer?（Tom 今年夏天要做什麼？）

　　· He's going to take a trip to China.（他要到中國去旅行。）

　　· What are you going to do tonight?（今晚你要做什麼？）

　　· I'm going to play computer games.（我要玩電腦遊戲。）

2.　第十一課的「現在完成式」談到問一個人的經驗：

　　· Has Tom ever been to China?（Tom 曾經去過中國嗎？）

　　· No, he hasn't. He has never been to China.（沒有，他從來沒有去過中國。）

3.　第十八課談到 must 這個助動詞，must 表「一定」的意味。注意助動詞後面要用動詞原形 be 。

　　excite 是動詞：This trip excites me.（這趟旅行令我興奮。）

　　你也可以說：

　　· I am excited about this trip.（我對這趟旅行感到興奮。）

　　· 可以想見這趟旅行一定會很刺激：This trip should be exciting.

　　注意：excite 的名詞是 excitement 。

4.　這個句子有一點長，讀者不要怕，它是第十四章談到的「過去進行式」的用法。

　　請看例句：

　　· When he called me last night, I was taking a shower.

　　（昨晚他打電話給我時，我正在洗澡。）

　　· When the teacher walked into the classroom, many students were sleeping.

（老師走進教室時，很多學生正在睡覺。）

5.　這句用被動的方式呈現（第十五課：was written by）。請注意第 4 句用 a novel，第 5 句用 the novel。novel 第一次在文章中出現時，表示某一本小說，用 "a"；第二次出現時，指的就是 Mary 手中的這一本，用 "the"。同樣的，a Chinese writer 我們不知道作者大名，只知道是某位中國作家。

6.　interest 是動詞也是名詞，請看例句：

　・This movie interests me.（這部電影讓我覺得有興趣。）

　・I have a great interest in this movie.（我對這部電影有極大的興趣。）

你也可以說：

　・I am interested in this movie.（我對這部電影很有興趣。）

因為 This movie looks very interesting.（這部電影看起來很有趣。）

注意：介系詞 in 後面的動詞要改成動名詞：be interested in reading。

7.　bore 是動詞也是名詞，請看例句：

　・Mike is a bore. He talks all the time.（Mike 是個無聊的傢伙，他一直講個不停。）

　・Watching TV bores me.（看電視讓我覺得很無聊。）

也可以說：

　・I am bored of watching TV.（我覺得看電視真無聊。）

　・Watching TV is boring.（看電視真無聊。）

注意：be bored with ＝ be bored of；介系詞後面的動詞要改成動名詞：be bored of reading ／ be bored with reading。

8.　like 後面可以接不定詞：like to travel，也可以接動名詞：like traveling。

9.　How often 的用法請看第十八課的解說。注意：在 "does Mary read novels" 中，read 雖接在第三人稱 Mary 後面，卻要用原形，不加 s，因為前面

有助動詞 does，助動詞後面接原形動詞。第 10 句 Mary reads novels.
是肯定句，read 要加 s。

10. once a week（一星期一次）、 twice a week（一星期兩次）、 three times
a week（一星期三次）……。

範文二

 生字

busy	忙
just	剛剛
important	重要的
report	報告
visit	拜訪
room	房間
messy	髒亂
make the bed	鋪床
do the dishes	洗碗
had better	最好
clean	清理、打掃(clean, cleaned, cleaned)
right now	當下,現在

Amy will be very busy today.[1] Last night when her friends called her, she was doing her homework.[2] They told her they had just finished an important report.[3] They will visit her tonight.[4] Amy's room is very messy.[5] She must make the bed and do the dishes before they come.[6] What time will her friends come?[7] They may come at 7:30 P.M.[8] Amy had better clean her room right now.[9]

翻譯

今天Amy會很忙。昨晚她的朋友打電話給她時,她正在做功課, 他們告訴她,他們剛完成一個重要的報告,今天晚上會來拜訪她。 Amy的房間很亂,他們來之前她得鋪床和洗碗。她的朋友什麼時候會 來?他們也許會在晚上 7 點半來。Amy 最好現在就打掃她的房間。

課文解析

1. 顯然今天才剛開始，可以預見 Amy 今天會很忙，所以得用未來式：will be busy 。

2. 這句跟範文一的第 4 句結構相同，請參看。
   They told her 是昨晚打電話時說的，而他們完成一份重要的報告比打電話還要超前，比過去還要過去，所以得用過去完成式：had finished（請看第十三課）。注意：important 字首的發音／ɪ／是母音，a 要改為 an 。

3. 今晚還沒有到，得用未來式。

4. messy 是形容詞，mess 是名詞，Her room is always messy. 也可以說 Her room is always in a mess.

5. 請看第十九課 must 的用法。

6. 用未來式問 Amy 朋友到達的時間。

7. 用 may 來表示朋友到的時間並不確定。

8. had better 的用法請看第十九課，注意 had better 後面的動詞用原形。

範文三

生字

rain	下雨（rain, rained, rained）
buy	買（buy, bought, bought）
at	在（介系詞）
bookstore	書店
umbrella	雨傘
borrow	（向某人）借（borrow, borrowed, borrowed）
behind	在後面
in front of	在前面
lend	借給（別人）（lend, lent, lent）
quickly	快（副詞）
if	如果

It's raining now.[1] David has to buy an English book at the bookstore.[2] He doesn't have an umbrella.[3] He must borrow Jane's.[4] Where is Jane's umbrella?[5] It's behind the door.[6] Jane can't lend hers to him for too long.[7] She has to meet her friend in front of the department store this afternoon.[8] David had better come back quickly. Does David have a cell phone?[9] We should call him if he has one.[10]

翻譯

現在正在下雨，David 必須到書店買一本英文書，他沒有雨傘，他必須借 Jane 的。 Jane 的雨傘在哪？它在門的後面。 Jane 不能借她的傘給他太久，今天下午她必須在百貨公司門口見她的朋友。David 最好快點回來，David 有手機嗎？如果他有，我們應該打給他。

課文解析

1. 現在發生的事用「現在進行式」。

2. 參看第十九課 have to 的用法。English 字首發音是母音，所以 a 要改為 an。

　動詞 have 的否定，是在動詞前面加 doesn't。doesn't 後面動詞用原形 have 而不用第三人稱的 has。

3. 參看第十九課 must 的用法，注意：must 後面用動詞原形 borrow，must 後面絕對不能加 to。Jane's 代表 Jane's umbrella。

4. 參看第二十二課找東西。Jane 的所有格是 Jane's。umbrella 是單數，所以用 Where is，如果 umbrellas 是複數，be 動詞也跟著變：Where are Jane's umbrellas?

5. It's 是 It is 的縮寫，代名詞 it 代表 Jane's umbrella。

6. 注意 borrow 和 lend 的意思雖都是「借」，意思卻不同。hers 是所有代名詞，意指 Jane's umbrella(參看第二課)。for too long，for 用來表達一段時間的介系詞。

7. quickly 是形容動作 come back 的副詞(參看第八課的詞類變化)。

8. 第三人稱動詞問句的用法：Does he have a cell phone?
　Yes, he does. He has a cell phone.

9. 假設語氣 if(如果)，"If he has one," 裡的 one 指的是 a cell phone。
　should 的用法請看第十九課。

總複習

I. 選擇題

1.　(　) Yesterday they were hungry because they (1)hadn't eaten　(2) haven't eaten　(3)didn't eat　for four hours.

2.　(　) (1) After　(2) Before　(3) If　she went to America, she had already learned some English.

3.　(　) We (1) are　(2) had been　(3) were　late. The party had already started.

4.　(　) My parents (1) are taking a nap　(2)took a nap　(3)were taking a nap when I came home at 1 o'clock.

5.　(　) Your sister (1) was writting　(2) was writing　(3) had written　a novel when her boyfriend called her last night.

6.　(　) This novel (1) has written　(2) had written　(3) was written　by my sister.

7.　(　) This e-mail (1) is send　(2) has sent　(3) was sent　by my teacher.

8.　(　) My cousins (1) are going　(2) will go　(3) are going to　buy some socks, T-shirts, and blue jeans.

9.　(　) I didn't know you (1) were interesting in　(2) interested in　(3) were interested in　baseball games.

10.　(　) How often (1) are　(2)were　(3) do　you and your sister go to the museum?

11.　(　) They exercise (1) three time　(2) three times　(3)third time　a week.

12. （　）My sister seldom (1) cooks (2) cook (3) cooking because she is very busy.

13. （　）You had better not (1) to buy (2) bought (3) buy that expensive purple T-shirt.

14. （　）You must (1) to take a shower (2) take a shower (3) have taken a shower before you go to bed.

15. （　）You (1) should be (2) have to (3) have better talk to your teacher tomorrow.

16. （　）Your mom looked wonderful (1) on (2) in (3) at the picture.

17. （　）I (1) borrow (2) lend (3) lent Tom some money yesterday.

18. （　）Let her (2) calls (2) to call (3) call her mom first, we can talk to her later.

19. （　）Excuse me, could you tell me where (1) is the art museum? (2) are the art museum? (3) the art museum is?

20. （　）I don't know (1) where do you put my watch? (2) where you put my watch. (3) where is my watch.

II. 填充題

1. My sister _____ (write) a letter to the writer before she met him.

2. We weren't hungry because we _____ (eat) some cakes.

3. I didn't know him. I _____ never _____ (see) him before.

4. John _____ (talk) to his girlfriend on the phone when I came in.

5. When Amy _____ (meet) Tom, she was living in America.

6. This English book _____ (write) by my teacher.

7. The important report should_____ (finish) tonight.

8. I _____ (tell, told, told 被告知) about this popular singer's interesting story.

9. She was bored of_____ (read) that long novel.

10. Tom has a great interest _____ playing computer games.

11. I seldom visit art museums. I'm not _____ (interest) in art (藝術).

12. I'm going to_____ (buy) a computer tomorrow.

13. Who _____going to go to the science museum with me?

14. How often do you go _____ (swim)?

15. My dad seldom _____ (exercise) because he is too busy.

16. I bought this teddy bear _____the department store.

17. The T-shirt is too expensive. You _____buy it. (不應該)

18. Let _____ (我們) finish our homework first, we can go there later.

19. I don't know where my sister's socks _____ (be).

20. Excuse me, _____you tell me where the ladies' room is?

III. 問答

1. Where was Amy when I called her yesterday morning?
   When you called Amy, she _____to school. (已經上學去了)。

2. Why was your grandma so excited at the party?
   She was excited because she _____ a party before. (從來沒去過)

3. Where were you at 7:30 last night?
   I _____ (dance) at the party.

4. What was Tom doing when his mom walked into his room?

He _____ (drink and smoke).

5. Who washed those dirty dishes?

    They _____ by my husband this afternoon.

6. Who sent you this e-mail?

    I don't know. Maybe it _____(send) by my student.

7. How was the movie?

    It's a very popular movie, but I found it _____.(無聊)

8. How did you like this famous computer game?

    I_____(surprise) to find it wasn't so good.

9. How often do you go shopping?

    I _____.(一個月三次)

10. How often do you go jogging?

    I _____.(從不慢跑)

11. What are you going to do this summer?

    I_____.(寫一本關於我自己的書)

12. What is your boyfriend going to do tonight?

    He_____.(去運動)

13. What are your parents going to do this afternoon?

    They_____ and do nothing.(待在家裡。)

14. Could you help me finish this work？

    I'm sorry, I_____ for my school newspaper.(必須幫
    學校報紙照相)

15. Which computer should I buy?

    You_____ that one because it's cheaper.(你最好買
    那台因為比較便宜。)

16. Do you mind if I borrow your bike?

I'm sorry, _____.（我剛借給 Mary 了）

17. What should we do now?

_____; we can go swimming later.（讓我們先打電話給她）

18. Where're my jeans?

They're_____.（在你的床下面）

19. Where's the art museum?

It's_____.（郵局的對面）

20. What time does the next show start?

It _____.（6:30 P.M 開始）

IV. 改錯

1. By the time they arrive, the train had already left.
2. Amy was excited because she has never been to a party before.
3. I brushed my teeth when my teacher visited me.
4. What are you doing when I called you thirty minutes ago?
5. The report will finish in a minute.
6. I was surprising at this bad news.
7. It was a long tired day today.
8. I'm exciting about the trip to China.
9. He's going to having a wonderful time at Kenting.
10. I don't know what are we going to do tomorrow.
11. How often do you go swiming?
12. My grandpa is health because he exercises every day.
13. You must to go to bed now. It's very late.
14. You had better not to eat this junk food（垃圾食物）.

15.   I let him to do the dishes for me.

16.   Do you mind if I lend your bike?

17.   Do you know where is my cell phone?

18.   I don't know where did you put your cell phone.

19.   Could you tell me what time is the next show?

20.   I shouldn't let him to use my computer. It's broken.

V. 英文該怎麼寫？

1.   我告訴他我已經看過那部電影了。

      I told him I _____

2.   他見那位有名的作家之前就已經讀過她的小說了。

      Before he met _____

3.   我到晚了，派對已經開始了 30 分鐘了。

      I was late. The party _____

4.   1987 年我正在台中教學生英文。

      In 1987 _____ in Taichung.

5.   你來拜訪我時，我正在睡午覺。

      When you visited _____

6.   我們對她的成就感到驚訝。

      We were _____ her success.

7.   他完成報告後累慘了。

      After he had finished the report _____

8.   你今年夏天計畫做什麼？

      This summer _____

9.   我計畫遊台灣一圈 (travel around Taiwan)。

      _____

10. 你最好讓他幫你照相(take pictures of you)。

     _____

11. 你的新牛仔褲太貴了，你不應該買的。

     Your new jeans _____

12. 下雨了，我最好趕快回家。

     It's raining _____ quickly.

13. 你介意我向你借這本小說嗎？

     Do you mind if _____

14. 我已經把腳踏車借給 Amy 了。

     I've already _____

15. 讓他先午睡，我們可以待會兒再慢跑。

     Let him _____

16. 讓我們一起來唱一首英文歌。

     Let's sing _____ together.

17. 你知道我的雨傘(umbrella)在哪裡？

     Do you know _____

18. 我不知道男廁所在哪裡。

     I don't know _____

19. 下班火車什麼時候離開(leave)？

     _____

20. 我有時間刷牙嗎？

     Do I have time _____

習題解答

第十三課

13-4-1 連接句子，其中一句用過去完成式

1. Before I went to bed, I had finished reading a novel.
2. My brother went to America after he had learned English.
3. My mother had done the dishes before she read a novel.
4. After she had finished her work, she wrote a letter.
5. Before David went home, he had called his father.
6. The teacher took a nap after he (或she) had had lunch.
7. My grandma made a cake after she had made cookies.
8. Yesterday, my sister had finished her homework before she went to school.
9. The English class had finished before those students arrived.
10. After my grandfather had seen a movie, he wrote letters to his friends.

13-4-2 填填看

1. had finished
2. had written
3. moved
4. had called
5. before
6. after
7. had finished
8. before
9. drink
10. before
11. before
12. had finished
13. had met
14. left
15. called

13-4-3 英文該怎麼說

1. Before he came to Taiwan, he had learned some Chinese.
2. I had bought a present before I met the new teacher.
3. Before I went to bed, I had finished my homework.
4. My brothers went to school after they had cleaned their bedroom.
5. I was not hungry last night because I had eaten dinner.
6. Before he moved to Taipei last year, he had lived in Taichung for three years.
7. My friend and I had finished our homework before we watched TV.
8. After my grandma had eaten breakfast, she went to the park.
9. My students went to school after they had read books.
10. He had already read the novel before he saw the movie.

13-4-4 改錯

1. have → had
2. start → started
3. knew → known
4. see → had seen
5. have → had
6. already started → had already started
7. arrive → arrived
8. After → Before
9. are → were
10. After → Before

第十四課

14-3-1 你在做什麼（參考答案）

1. was brushing my teeth
2. was studying English
3. was doing the dishes
4. was watching TV
5. was taking a shower

14-3-2 填填看

1. have been learning
2. study
3. was taking
4. had gone
5. has
6. will be
7. was doing
8. had bought

9. had talked

10. decided

11. doing

12. was making

13. was reading

14. found

15. care

14-3-3 改錯

1. take → taking

2. isn't → wasn't

3. study → studying

4. sleep → sleeping

5. are → were

6. takeing → taking

7. wasn't → weren't

8. didn't → wasn't

9. read → reading

10. are → were

第十五課

15-3-1 選選看

1. (2)

2. (3)

3. (2)

4. (3)

5. (1)

6. (3)

7. (2)

8. (3)

9. (2)

10. (1)

11. (3)

12. (2)

13. (3)

14. (3)

15. (2)

15-3-2 換成被動語態說說看

2. I was given a present by my teacher yesterday.

3. This letter was written by my father yesterday.

4. The window was broken by my brother.

5. These e-mails were sent to her friends by Amy.

6. My homework was finished by me at 8 o'clock.

7. The car was washed by David for his father this afternoon.

8. The windows were washed by my sister yesterday.

9. The house was cleaned by my brother and me last week.

10. The lunch was made by my grandparents for us yesterday.

11. This picture was painted by him last night.

12. The book was finished reading by Amy this afternoon.

13. This novel was written by her last year.

14. Some e-mails are often written by me to my friends.

15. Tom's bed is made by himself every morning.

15-3-3 英文該怎麼說

1. will be washed by Amy

2. was broken by his student(s)

3. were given, by those students

4. was made by my brother

5. was made by my student(s)

6. was finished by him(self)

7. were broken by my cat

8. was written by my father

9. was drunk by my cat

10. was sent by my teacher

11. was painted by my grandpa

12. has been played by us

13. has been read by my grandma

14. was seen by the nurses last night

15. was found by the doctor yesterday

第十六課

16-5-1 填填看（ing 還是 ed）

1. interesting, interested

2. boring, bored

3. excited, exciting

4. tiring, tired

5. surprised, surprising

6. interested

7. excited

8. boring

9. tiring

10. surprised

16-5-2 選選看

1. (2)

2. (1)

3. (3)

4. (1)

5. (3)

6. (2)

7. (1)

8. (3)

9. (2)

10. (2)

16-5-3 英文該怎麼說

1. She is a popular singer in Taiwan.

2. My mom is bored of this stupid book.

3. Amy has written a popular novel.

4. My father was surprised to hear the terrible news.

5. I'm excited about going to America. (或I'm excited to go to America.)

6. My brother had a tiring week.

7. It's interesting to make cookies.

8. I'm interested in cooking.

9. David is bored because he is reading a boring book.

10. This news is surprising to my family.

16-5-4 改錯

1. exciting → excited

2. interesting → interested

3. tiring → tired

4. of → in

5. listen → listening

6. hearing → hear

7. seeing → see

8. exciting → excited

9. do → doing

10. make → making

第十七課

17-4-1 選選看

1. (2)

2. (1)

3. (3)

4. (1)

5. (3)

6. (2)

7. (3)

8. (2)

9. (3)

10. (2)

17-4-2 問答題

1. I'm going to see a friend.

2. She's going to watch a baseball game.

3. She's going to go shopping.

4. He's going to call his parents.

5. They're going to play cards.

6. She's going to make cookies.

7. We're going to drink coffee together.

8. They're going to read novels.

9. He's going to do his homework.

10. He's going to take a nap.

17-4-3 看圖回答問題

2. She's going to buy some flowers.

3. She's going to buy a bottle of milk.

4. She's going to buy two skirts.

5. She's going to buy a pair of jeans.

6. She's going to buy two T-shirts.

7. She's going to buy five mangos.

8. She's going to buy a piece of pork.

9. She's going to buy some books.

10. She's going to buy some eggs.

17-4-4 改錯

1. will → is

2. eating → eat

3. buy → to buy

4. will → am

5. does → is

6. is → are

7. will → are

8. is → are

9. see → to see

10. reading → read

第十八課

18-4-1 填填看

1. walks the dog

2. sometimes

3. no wonder

4. twice a year

5. goes jogging

6. How often

7. kind of

8. three times a week

9. twice a month

10. too busy

11. art museum

12. science museum

13. not interested

14. going

15. tired

18-4-2 請根據自己的情況回答下列問題

1. I seldom go to the museum.

2. I go shopping once a month.

3. I never buy milk.

4. I listen to music every day.

5. He hardly ever does the dishes.

6. I seldom read novels.

7. I exercise twice a day.

8. I brush my teeth three times a day.

9. I go swimming once a year.

10. I hardly ever see a movie.

18-4-3 英文該怎麼說

1. David goes to the museum three times a month.

2. My dad goes to the department store twice a week.

3. I go swimming three times a week.

4. My sister seldom cooks because she is too busy.

5. He exercises every day; no wonder he looks so healthy.

6. My cat sometimes breaks bowls.

7. I walk the dog in the park every day.

8. How often do you exercise?

9. My children brush their teeth twice a day.

10. My English teacher goes to school five times a week.

11. My grandpa takes a walk in the park three times a week.

12. Her grandparents go to Japan once a year.

13. His brother is bored of walking the dog every day.

14. She is interested in sports.

15. Amy hardly ever exercises.

第十九課

19-4-1 選選看

1. (2)

2. (2)

3. (1)

4. (1)

5. (3)

6. (2)

7. (1)

8. (3)

9. (2)

10. (1)

19-4-2 填填看

1. Wait a minute

2. Not really

3. cute, at

4. must, take a rest

5. had better, should（must）

6. have to, safer

19-4-3 英文該怎麼說

1. Should I buy this pair of expensive jeans?

2. This teacher took a taxi to school.

3. I have to call my grandparents tonight.

4. You mustn't watch TV now.

5. Your dad had better exercise three times a week.

6. Your sisters look cute.

7. I think I should make the bed now.

8. Is it safe to take a taxi at night?

9. I have to brush my teeth three times a day.

10. My mom must take a rest this afternoon.

19-4-4 改錯

1. must → has（或 to 去掉）

2. to 去掉

3. must → has（或 to 去掉）

4. had → have

5. must → have（或 to 去掉）

6. to 去掉

7. at → on

8. to 去掉

9. has → have

10. it is → they are

第二十課

20-3-1 填填看

1. borrow, I'm sorry

2. mind, not at all

3. take a look, Go ahead

4. wonderful

5. take a picture

6. lend

7. in a minute

20-3-2 用 lend 還是 borrow

1. borrow

2. lent

3. borrowed

4. borrowed

5. lend

6. borrow

7. lend

8. lend

9. lend

10. borrow

20-3-3 改錯

1. lend → borrow

2. in → at

3. took → take

4. at → in

5. lend → borrow

6. to → from（或 borrowed → lent）

7. to 去掉

8. takes → took

9. borrow → borrowed

10. few → a few

20-3-4 想一想再回答（參考答案）

1. No, not at all.

2. No, I don't mind at all.

3. No, I love singing.

4. Yes, it's boring and tiring to do my homework every day.

5. Yes, I never go to bed after twelve o'clock.

6. Yes, because I can't play it well.

7. Yes, that's my brother's job.

8. Yes, loud music tires me.

9. No, I don't like playing computer games at all.

10. It depends.（視情況而定）

第二十一課

21-3-1 選選看

1. （2）

2. （1）

3. （3）

4. （2）

5. （3）

6. （1）

7. （3）

8. （2）

9. （2）

10. （1）

21-3-2 英文該怎麼說

1. Let him take a nap first.

2. Let her watch TV first; she can do the dishes later.

3. Let this student talk first; we can talk later.

4. I let her go first.

5. My mom always lets me take a shower first.

6. Let's go to Taipei tomorrow.

7. Let me take a look at your homework.

8. May I play computer games for a while?

9. What should we do now?

10. Did you buy pet food for your rabbit?

21-3-3 改錯

1. goes → go

2. does → do

3. reads → read

4. driving → drive

5. to 去掉

6. didn't → don't

7. to 去掉

8. doing → do

9. to 去掉

10. is look → looks

第二十二課

22-3-1 由直接問句變爲敘述句

1. is

2. is

3. are

4. is

5. is

6. are

7. are

8. are

9. is

10. is

22-3-2 填填看

1. on, in

2. in

3. either

4. next to

5. in front of

6. under

7. behind

8. it

9. disappear

10. they

22-3-3 英文該如何説

1. My grandma can't find her glasses.

2. This rabbit disappeared in front of my eyes.

3. The newspaper is under the tea table.

4. Maybe your T-shirt is in my bedroom.

5. I can't see this bird, either.

6. Where is my watch?

7. My brother has three bookshelves in his bedroom.

（或 There are three bookshelves in my brother's bedroom.）
8. My dog likes to sit next to me.
9. Please put the cake on the table.
10. I don't know where you put the bowl(s).

第二十三課

23-3-1 填填看
1. welcome
2. repeat
3. Excuse me, see
4. Pardon
5. turn
6. still
7. across
8. next
9. see
10. Don't worry

23-3-2 中文該怎麼說
1. Don't worry.
2. it is
3. worry, repeat
4. next to the post office
5. and then turn left

6. on your right
7. You're welcome.
8. at the post office
9. Let me see.
10. across from

23-3-3 改錯
1. department → the department
2. in → at
3. at → on
4. is my pencil → my pencil is
5. is the ladies' room → the ladies' room is
6. will he → he will
7. is he → he is
8. park → the park
9. is 去掉
10. are → do（或 come 去掉）

第二十四課

24-3-1 選選看
1. （1）
2. （2）
3. （3）
4. （2）
5. （2）

6. (3)

7. (3)

8. (1)

9. (2)

10. (3)

24-3-2 填填看

1. What time is it

2. interested in

3. Let me check, about

4. leave, at

5. newspaper, Hurry up

24-3-3 英文該如何說

1. The next bus leaves at six ten.

2. You have to finish reading this novel in a week.

3. Are you interested in seeing a movie with me?

4. When does the next bus leave?

5. Have you bought today's newspaper?

6. What time does the next show start?

7. Have movie starts at seven thirty.

8. What time is it now?

9. Let me check today's newspaper.

10. Which movie do you want to see?

24-3-4 改錯

1. is → does

2. must → have（或 to 去掉）

3. readed → read

4. is start → starts

5. interesting → interested

6. Talk → Talking

7. play → playing

8. must → have（或 to 去掉）

9. is → does

10. does the movie start → the movie starts

總複習解答

I. 選擇題

1. (1)
2. (2)
3. (3)
4. (3)
5. (2)
6. (3)
7. (3)
8. (3)
9. (3)
10. (3)
11. (2)
12. (1)
13. (3)
14. (2)
15. (2)
16. (2)
17. (3)
18. (3)
19. (3)
20. (2)

II. 填充題

1. had written
2. had eaten
3. had, seen
4. was talking
5. met
6. was written
7. be finished
8. was told
9. reading
10. in
11. interested
12. buy
13. is
14. swimming
15. exercises
16. at
17. shouldn't
18. us
19. are
20. could

III. 問答

1. had already gone
2. had never been to
3. was dancing
4. was drinking and smoking
5. were washed
6. was sent
7. was boring
8. was surprised
9. go shopping three times a month
10. never go jogging
11. am going to write a book about myself
12. is going to exercise
13. are going to stay at home
14. have to take pictures
15. had better buy
16. I've just lent it to Mary
17. Let's call her first
18. under your bed
19. across from the post office
20. starts at 6:30P.M.

IV. 改錯

1. arrive → arrived
2. has → had
3. brushed → was brushing
4. are → were
5. finish → be finished
6. surprising → surprised
7. tired → tiring
8. exciting → excited
9. having → have
10. are we → we are
11. swiming → swimming
12. health → healthy
13. to 去掉（或 must 改為 have）
14. to 去掉
15. to 去掉
16. lend → borrow
17. is my cell phone → my cell phone is
18. did 去掉
19. is the next show → the next show is
20. to 去掉

V. 英文該怎麼寫？

1. I told him I had already seen that movie.
2. Before he met that famous writer,

he had already read her novels.

3. I was late. The party had already started for thirty minutes.

4. In 1987, I was teaching students English in Taichung.

5. When you visited me, I was taking a nap.

6. We were surprised at her success.

7. After he had finished the report, he was very tired.

8. This summer what are you going to do?

9. I'm going to travel around Taiwan.

10. You'd better let him take pictures of you.

11. Your new jeans are too expensive. You shouldn't buy them.

12. It's raining. I had better go home quickly.

13. Do you mind if I borrow this novel from you?

14. I've already lent the bike to Amy.

15. Let him take a nap first. We can go jogging later.

16. Let's sing an English song together.

17. Do you know where my umbrella is?

18. I don't know where the men's room is.

19. When does the next train leave?

20. Do I have time to brush my teeth?

從國人的需求出發的英文學習書

從中國人的需要出發的英文課本

破除現有英文課本的共同缺點　回歸學習英文的基本課程

初級本（上、下冊）

中級本（上、下冊）

高級本（上冊）

 聯經出版事業公司
www.linkingbooks.com.tw

郵政劃撥帳號：01005593　戶名：聯經出版事業公司
洽詢電話：02-2641-8662

從國人的需求出發的英文學習書

糾正中國人最容易犯錯的基本文法

專門替中國人寫的英文基本文法

李家同、海柏◎ 合著

如果你覺得,坊間的文法書太難了:讀完後文法還是不好;如果你真的想打下深厚的文法基礎,可是卻苦無門路,那麼,這本書就適合你。因為這本書是針對中國人最容易犯的文法錯誤所編寫的書!

我們兩人都有過教初級英文的經驗,我們發現我們中國人寫英文句子時,會犯獨特的錯誤,比方說,我們常將兩個動詞連在一起用,我們也會將動詞用成名詞,我們對過去式和現在式毫無觀念。更加不要說現在完成式了。而天生講英文的人是不可能犯這種錯的。

我們這本英文文法書,是專門為中國人寫的。以下是這本書的一些特徵:我們一開始就強調一些英文文法的基本規定,這些規定都是我們中國人所不太習慣的。也就是說,我們一開始就告訴了讀者,大家不要犯這種錯誤。

我們馬上就進入動詞,理由很簡單,這是我們中國人最弱的地方。根據我們的經驗,絕大多數的錯誤,都與動詞有關。這也難怪,中文裡面,哪有什麼動詞的規則?

最後我們要勸告初學的讀者,你們應該多多做練習,練習做多了,你自然不會犯錯。總有一天,你說英文的時候,動詞該加s,你就會加s。該用過去式,就會用過去式。兩個動詞也不會連在一起用,疑問句也會用疑問句的語法。那是多麼美好的一天。希望這一天早日到來!

李家同

海　柏

聯經出版事業公司
www.linkingbooks.com.tw

郵政劃撥帳號:01005593　戶名:聯經出版事業公司
洽詢電話:02-2641-8662

創意十足的英文教學指南

如何教小學生學英文

Wendy A. Scott &
Lisbeth H. Ytreberg 著
文庭澍譯

掌握學習英文的角度，提供許多教育理念和豐富的點子與活動。

全家學英文

文庭澍、傅凱　合著

以親子一日生活為經，父母與子女間互動為緯，中間穿插與文化相關的提示。整套書包括：親子學習書、兒童勞作書及CD。

 聯經出版事業公司
www.linkingbooks.com.tw

郵政劃撥帳號：01005593　戶名：聯經出版事業公司
洽詢電話：02-2641-8662

專門替中國人寫的英文課本　中級本（下冊）

2004年8月初版
2006年8月初版第六刷
2007年1月二版
2019年5月二版九刷
有著作權・翻印必究
Printed in Taiwan.

定價：新臺幣200元

著　　　者	文	庭	澍
策劃・審訂	李	家	同
叢書主編	何	采	嬪
校　　　對	林	慧	如
	海		柏
	Yvonne Yeh		
封面設計	陳	泰	榮
插　　　圖	陳	玉	嵐

出　版　者	聯經出版事業股份有限公司	總　編　輯	胡　金　倫
地　　　址	新北市汐止區大同路一段369號1樓	總　經　理	陳　芝　宇
台北聯經書房	台北市新生南路三段94號	社　　　長	羅　國　俊
電　　　話	（ 0 2 ） 2 3 6 2 0 3 0 8	發　行　人	林　載　爵
台中分公司	台中市北區崇德路一段198號		
暨門市電話	（ 0 4 ） 2 2 3 1 2 0 2 3		
郵政劃撥帳戶第0100559-3號			
郵 撥 電 話	（ 0 2 ） 2 3 6 2 0 3 0 8		
印　刷　者	世和印製企業有限公司		
總　經　銷	聯合發行股份有限公司		
發　行　所	新北市新店區寶橋路235巷6弄6號2F		
電　　　話	（ 0 2 ） 2 9 1 7 8 0 2 2		

行政院新聞局出版事業登記證局版臺業字第0130號

本書如有缺頁，破損，倒裝請寄回台北聯經書房更換。ISBN　978-957-08-3121-4 (平裝附光碟)
聯經網址 http://www.linkingbooks.com.tw
電子信箱 e-mail:linking@udngroup.com

國家圖書館出版品預行編目資料

專門替中國人寫的英文課本　中級本
（下冊）／文庭澍著．李家同策劃・審訂．
二版．新北市：聯經，2007年（民96）
160面；19×26公分．
ISBN　978-957-08-3121-4(平裝附光碟片)
[2019年5月二版九刷]

1.英國語言 －讀本

805.18　　　　　　　　　　　　　96001386